APR 08

CH

THE BABY
ON THE WAY

Karen English
Pictures by Sean Qualls

Farrar Straus Giroux
New York

For each of my children—Ain, Kenneth, Erin, Isaac—
who were once the baby on the way
—K.E.

To my wife, Selina, and our baby on the way
—S.Q.

Text copyright © 2005 by Karen English
Illustrations copyright © 2005 by Sean Qualls
Distributed in Canada by Douglas & McIntyre Publishing Group
Color separations by Embassy Graphics
Printed and bound in the United States of America by Phoenix Color Corporation
Designed by Barbara Grzeslo
First edition, 2005
1   3   5   7   9   10   8   6   4   2

www.fsgkidsbooks.com

Library of Congress Cataloging-in-Publication Data
English, Karen.
    The baby on the way / Karen English ; pictures by Sean Qualls.— 1st ed.
        p. cm.
    Summary: A young boy asks his grandmother if she was ever a baby; she tells
him the story of how she was born.
    ISBN-13: 978-0-374-37361-0
    ISBN-10: 0-374-37361-2
    [1. Grandmothers—Fiction.   2. Babies—Fiction.   3. African Americans—
Fiction.]   I. Qualls, Sean, ill.   II. Title.

PZ7.E7232Sw 2005
[E]—dc21

                                                            2003049047

Just after the sun had slipped behind the rooftops and the air had stilled, Jamal brushed the dirt from his palms and looked up at Grandma hard.

"Grandma," he said soft as a whisper, because a question had suddenly blossomed.

"What, baby?"

"Were you ever a little girl?"

Grandma laughed. "A little girl . . . Why yes, I was a little girl—once."

Jamal looked and looked at Grandma.

"Grandma," he said after a while. "Were you a baby, too?"

Grandma smiled. "I sure was. Your ol' grandma was even once *the baby on the way*."

"What's that?"

"The baby comin'. Just like you were once," Grandma said.

She put the last tomato in the basket and took Jamal by the hand to go inside.

In the kitchen, while preparing a fresh garden salad, Grandma said, "Oh yes . . . I was quite an event.

"When my mama's time come, Big Sis ran all the way down to the lower field from the house to tell my daddy, 'It's time!'

" 'Go get Aunt Nannie,' Daddy told Big Sis. Aunt Nannie birthed us all.

"Big Sis, still in an apron covered in flour, hurried toward town.

"Then, Daddy left the plow in the field, hear tell, and ran all the way back to the house—most of it uphill.

"Big Sis arrived on Aunt Nannie's porch breathless and unable to speak for seconds. Finally, she got the news out, and they hurried back to the house together, Aunt Nannie with her birthin' bag full of secret things.

"She sent all the children who were home 'cept Big Sis down to Ma Blanche, my daddy's mama. Solemnly they left, the littlest ones knowin' something was up, but not knowin' what.

"Baby Christina cried. She was Mama's lap baby, gettin' ready to be passed on to Big Sis to become the knee baby.

"Daddy paced the porch and prayed. Ol' Beverly, our dog, looked on and whimpered. (Worried about Daddy, must've been.) Up and down, up and down, Daddy paced.

"Finally, I done arrived—screamin' loud enough to wake the whole county.

"All the children were called back to meet their new baby sister, Mama's tenth and, God willing, the last. Mama was so tired of havin' a baby a year, practically.

"They tiptoed in to stare down at me wrapped tightly in a blanket. Mama said I looked right back at 'em, and me just a few hours old.

"Aunt Nannie spread the word. I had finally come.

"One by one, neighbor women brought food and little things to help me get strong.

"My mama stayed in bed ten whole days. Then came the *takin' up ceremonies*—somethin' probably passed down from slavery times. People don't do that no more. Mama took me outside and carried me around the house seven times, singin' and prayin' all the while. Then, she drank water out of a thimble. Then, it was time to name me.

"Daddy wanted Minerva. Mama wanted Beatrice. They fussed and fussed over it, then settled on Beulah Rose.

"A couple of days later, an ol' neighbor woman came to smoke Mama's clothes in the fireplace so as to give my mama some strength where she was weak at."

Grandma laughed, almost to herself. "You know, my feet hardly touched the ground my whole first two years. I was carried everywhere. Just passed around from person to person.

" 'Give her what she wants,' Mama would say whenever I cried. She was tired by the tenth child.

"A man came by with a pony one day and I had my picture taken on that little pony—the onliest one in the family to ever get their picture taken on a pony. With a big yellow ribbon in my hair and a pretty yellow dress Mama had made by hand. 'Cause I was my mama and daddy's sweet little baby."

A dog outside howled at a siren going by. When the noise died away, Grandma said, "What do you think of that?"

Jamal didn't know what to think.

Except . . .

"Grandma—do you think one day somebody will ask if I was ever a baby?"

"Yes, sweetheart. If you should live so long—one day your grandchild will say, 'Grandpa Jamal, was you ever a baby?' " Grandma put her arms around him. "And what will you tell 'em?"

"That I was once the baby on the way?"

"Oh yes," Grandma said. "And I know all about it. Shall I tell it to you?"